BOY ZERO
WANNABE HERO

THE ATTACK OF THE BRAIN-DEAD BREAKDANCING ZOMBIES

Peter Millett

Illustrations by Steve May

faber and faber

FOR RUTH

First published in 2010 by
Faber and Faber Limited
Bloomsbury House, 74–77 Great Russell Street,
London, WC1B 3DA

Typeset by Faber and Faber
Printed in England by CPI BookMarque, Croydon

A CIP record for this book
is available from the British Library

ISBN 978–0–571–25323–4

2 4 6 8 10 9 7 5 3 1

CONTENTS

v

AUTHOR NOTE

One spider was slightly injured during the making of this book.

(I think he's recovered now.)

SUPERHERO OR SUPER SCAREDY-CAT?

Charlie Applejack, the galaxy's most exciting new superhero, once again found himself trapped in the clutches of an evil villain about to destroy the earth.

Smiling, Emperor Gorticus coiled his tail around his spiky collar and pushed a button. **KERTHUMP!** A gigantic Cyclops descended from the sky.

'Prepare to face your doom, Zero Boy!' The emperor chortled.

'My name's Hero Boy, you snake-eyed scumbag,' Charlie bellowed, raising his fists.

FIZOW! FIZOW! Laser bolts blasted from its pulsing eye. Charlie dodged left and right, narrowly avoiding each scorching ray. He rolled over on to his back, grabbed the Cyclops by its leg and, with a **HUMPHH!** sent it flying towards the horizon.

Emperor Gorticus pushed another button. *SPRONG.* Three diamond-shaped objects popped up into the air and began to spray Charlie with spitting fireballs.

Charlie dived to the ground. Suddenly he felt his nose itching. **KER-CHOO!** He exploded a thundering super sneeze, extinguishing the deadly fireballs.

'Most impressive,' Emperor Gorticus boomed. 'But tell me, just how are you going to cope with *this* little number?' The evil villain opened his claws, revealing a tiny hairy spider in the middle of his palm.

Charlie collapsed to his knees. 'No . . . no . . . not a . . . s-s-spider! Not a little hairy s-s-spider! NO!!!'

'Muhaa-hhaa.' Opening his jaws, Emperor Gorticus moved in for the kill.

Just then a blinding light stung Charlie's eyes.

'Huh?' Charlie sat bolt upright in his bed. He threw back his blankets and desperately searched for any sign of a spider.

'Charlie, what on earth's going on?' his mum asked, rushing into the bedroom.

Charlie rubbed the sleep from his eyes. 'Um, nothing, Mum. I think I just had another spider nightmare.'

Mum put her hands on her hips.

'Honestly, Charlie, I think you must be stressed. Maybe it's time you changed careers. I don't see how you can make a success of being a superhero if you're still scared of something as small and as silly as a spider.'

'Mum, spiders aren't all small,' Charlie said. 'Once I saw a spider that was nearly as big as my thumb.'

Mum sighed. 'Listen, Charlie, have you ever

thought about becoming a dentist? I hear that
dentists have fabulous houses, and that they always
get to drive the best-looking sports cars. And
you're hardly ever likely to bump into a spider in a
dentist's surgery, are you?'

Charlie groaned and sunk his head back into
his pillow. But as he lay there he felt something
hairy brush up against his ear. His face turned
whiter than the pillow case. Looking slowly to his
right, he saw a long hairy leg poking out from
under his pillow.

'Argh!! S-s-s-spider! Spider!!!' Charlie jumped
out of bed and – **KERSLAM** – smashed into
the ceiling, then bounced back down to the floor.

'Argh! There's a spider in my bed!'

Charlie's dad popped his head round the door.
'Hey, son, what's all the commotion going on in
here?'

Charlie pointed at the pillow, barely able to
move. 'D-Dad, there's a s-spider in my bed. Help!
G-get rid of it.'

Dad put his hands on his hips and frowned.

'I think what we have here is another important

life-learning lesson. Son, what you're experiencing right now is a powerful human emotion called fear. This emotion can cause your heart rate to increase, your nervous system to shut down, and your stomach to turn inside out – much like the after-effects of eating a dodgy curry. During my research for my number-one bestselling book *If You Can't Stand the Heat in the Kitchen – Then Open a Window* I learned some valuable tips about controlling fear from the brave warriors of the Meemeegoweewee tribe, who lived in the jungles of Uangadunadoo.'

He tiptoed quietly over to the pillow. 'Once, these warriors suffered from a terrible fear of a gigantic crocodile that lived in the forest near their village – but now, incredibly, they have absolutely no fear of the crocodile.'

'Really?' Charlie said. 'How did they overcome their fear?'

'It was simple, Charlie. The warriors decided the easiest way to beat their fear of the crocodile was to show the creature that they were no longer afraid of it, and that the crocodile should actually fear them. Each warrior would kneel in front of its massive jaws, stick his fingers up his nose and loudly chant "mee-mee-go-wee-wee" three times, to show it who was boss.'

'Man, that's awesome,' marvelled Charlie. 'What did the crocodile do after the warriors kneeled in front of its wide-open jaws, stuck their fingers up their noses, and chanted "mee-mee-go-wee-wee" three times?'

MEE-MEE -GO-WEE-WEE!

'I have no idea,' Dad replied. 'During the entire time I spent observing the Meemeegoweewee tribe, I never once saw any of their warriors return alive from the forest.'

'Oh . . .'

Dad bent down over the pillow. He stuck his fingers up his nose and chanted 'mee-mee-go-wee-wee' three times. He slowly lifted up the pillow, then quickly jumped back.

'Oh, by jingo, look at the size of that brute!' he wailed. 'It's a beast!'

Charlie covered his eyes.

Just then Charlie's sister's cat, Mr Tiddlebink, leapt up on the bed and caught the spider between his teeth. He shook it back and forth then flung it across the room. BOING. The spider bounced off a wall, then – BOING – bounced off a mirror, and – BOING – landed on the floor, wobbling around in circles.

Mum pointed at the spider. 'Look – it's not real. It's made of rubber.'

Dad bent down and picked the rubbery spider off the floor. Charlie heaved a sigh of relief.

'See, Charlie,' Dad said. 'Sometimes the things we fear the most in life are simply not worth fearing at all.'

Charlie inspected the rubber spider. He stared at his sister. 'Hey, Trixie, do you know how this ended up in my bed?'

Trixie, shrugged her shoulders, barely containing her laughter.

'No . . . I have absolutely no idea who slipped that spider under your pillow last night, five minutes after you went to sleep.'

Later, after breakfast, Charlie raced back to his bedroom to put on his superhero costume. He fastened his shower curtain round his neck, slipped on his washing-up gloves and placed his swimming goggles over his eyes. He posed in front of the mirror, thrusting his arm out powerfully.

'Look out, bad guys,' he boomed. 'Hero Boy is coming to take you down!'

Just then, Mum poked her head round the door. 'Ah, Charlie, I know you're heading out, but before you go, would you mind being a sweetie and help Dad wash my car?'

Charlie's shoulders slumped. 'Um, okay . . .'

THE RiSE OF THE BRAiN-DEAD BREAKDANCiNG ZOMBiES

Later that day, a short man with an enormous nose dressed from head to toe in black paced about impatiently in a small room. The evil villain known as General Pandemonium was preparing to unleash the first phase of his most deadly plan yet to take over the planet.

A bright orange light flashed above the door of the windowless room.

'We're ready for you now,' came a voice over the intercom.

'Good.' The general clicked his heels together and stormed out of the room. He marched purposefully down a long corridor with his fists tightly clenched and his jaw clenched even tighter. He stopped at a large door. The door automatically swung open and there standing in front of him was a young woman holding a clipboard and a roll of stickers.

'Hey, great to see you,' said the young woman. 'My name's Jasmine.' She slapped a sticker on the general's chest. 'Okay, so you're the last contestant today and your number is 1138.' She pointed to her left. 'Now, just pop over there and see Susie and she'll show you where to go next.'

The general stared at her coldly. 'Susie, you say?'

He marched over to a tall woman dressed in white.

'Okay, great – you've got your identification sticker, you've got your fancy dress costume, and you've even brought your own microphone too! My, you're certainly one of the best-prepared contestants we've seen today.' Susie patted the general on his shoulder. 'All right, you'll be live on TV in fifteen seconds' time. Good luck and knock 'em dead.'

Susie walked off. While no one was looking, the

general quickly pulled out a blond wig from his inside his jacket and slipped it on his head.

'Five seconds . . .' called a stage hand from the corner. 'Three, two, one . . .'

The curtain parted and the studio audience clapped and cheered wildly.

'Welcome to *World's Greatest Pop Singer*, the show where tomorrow's stars appear today!' boomed the announcer's voice over the loudspeakers. Coloured lights flashed around the studio and production assistants ran up and down the aisles whipping the crowd into a frenzy.

Celebrity judge Cindy Fizzwick waved at the general. 'Hello, can you tell us your name, please?'

'Ah, sure, my name is Pand—' The general paused for a moment. 'Um, er, sorry, my name is . . . Andy.'

'Hi, Andy, great to meet you. Now, tell us why you want to be a contestant on *World's Greatest Pop Singer*?'

The general stared straight ahead. 'Just one reason, Cindy – world domination.'

Cindy slapped the desk and rocked about in her

chair. 'Ha-ha, I love your attitude, Andy. Good for you, it's great to see a singer with big goals.'

Damon Scowl, the world's nastiest celebrity judge, leaned into his microphone. 'Can I just say one thing, Andy? If you've got a voice anywhere near as big as that nose of yours, then you're going to win this competition easily.'

'Ha ha ha ha ha . . .' the audience erupted with laughter.

The general reached behind his back to grab his hidden laser blaster. A shrill voice burst through on

his earpiece.

'General, sir, don't do it,' Lieutenant Kurse cried from a secret location inside the building. 'Don't vaporise Damon Scowl live on TV. If the producers of the show discover that you're a supervillain and not a pop singer, it could badly affect your chances of winning the competition.'

Reluctantly, the general released his grip on his laser blaster and glared at Damon.

Celebrity judge Ronnie Razzledazzle stood up and waved his hands in the air. 'Hey, Andy, what's up, dog? What's happening, my man?'

The general looked blankly at Ronnie.

Ronnie beamed a big golden-toothed grin. 'Listen, pooch, pay no attention to that jive-talking bad-boy Damon Scowl. He's just dissin' you with whack, my brother. Now grab the stick and hit us with some *chillin fillin*, you hear?'

The general scratched his head. 'What on earth did you say just now?'

Ronnie's face fell and he sat down again. 'Um, can you sing us a song, please.'

The general nodded. 'Of course.'

14

The background lights dimmed and a hush fell over the audience.

'Andy, tell us what song you've chosen to sing for us tonight.' Cindy quizzed, batting her eyelids.

'Ah, tonight, Cindy, I'm going to sing a song that means a great deal to me. It's called "I'll Make You My Slave".'

'Oh, super.' Cindy said clapping her hands. 'It sounds lovely.'

The general clicked a strange-looking button at the base of his microphone. Suddenly – **BOOM-DA-DA-DA-BOOM** – the studio pulsed with a thumping electronic beat. 'Oh, just don't mis-behave – just surrender . . . and be my slave . . .' he warbled into the microphone.

Immediately the audience leapt to their feet and their right arms shot out and snaked wildly up and down through the air. A few seconds later their left arms shot out and started doing the same. Then their bodies jerked and jolted uncontrollably and they began shaking like out-of-control robots.

'Sir, it's working!' Lieutenant Kurse bellowed through the general's earpiece. 'The Break-o-

Tron mind-controlling system is working. The audience is completely under your spell. They're being transformed into brain-dead breakdancing zombies right before our very eyes!'

The general grinned and struck a rock-star pose in front of the cameras.

A few minutes later he finished singing his song, but despite the momentary silence the audience kept dancing energetically. The general walked over to the judge's panel. He lifted the microphone to his lips and stared at Cindy Fizzwick.

'*Say yes!*' he boomed.

Cindy bounced around in her seat and shouted 'Yes!' at the top of her lungs. Suddenly a giant purple smiley face appeared on the electronic screen on the front of the judges' desk.

The general turned to Ronnie Razzledazzle. '*Say yes!*' he bellowed.

Ronnie whooped and did a back flip. 'Yes!' he hollered. Another giant smiley face appeared below.

The general turned to Damon Scowl.

'*Say yes!*' he shouted.

But Damon Scowl didn't bat an eyelid. He just sat motionless, staring ahead into space.

'Sir, I don't understand what's happening,' Lieutenant Kurse whined. 'The Break-o-Tron doesn't seem to be working on Damon Scowl. Is it possible that he's not actually human?'

The general pressed his nose right up in into Damon Scowl's face. '*Say yes!*' he thundered.

Slowly, Damon Scowl's cheek muscles twitched. His head nodded slightly and his lips narrowly opened. 'Yes,' he said through gritted teeth.

Another smiley face appeared on the screen. 𝓐𝓞𝓞𝓞𝓖𝓖𝓐𝓐𝓐 – a siren sounded and 'Congratulations – you are through to the Quarter-Final!' flashed up on the screen in giant letters.

The smiling general switched off the strange-looking button on the base of his microphone and walked away from the stage.

'Awesome work, sir,' Lieutenant Kurse bubbled through his earpiece. 'You totally made that song your own!'

GOODNESS GRACIOUS GRANDPA!

After finishing his chores, Charlie spent the rest of the morning down at the park practising his flying skills.

His best friend Josh stood over a small skyrocket with a match in his hand. 'Okay, Charlie, as soon as this rocket launches you've got four seconds to grab it out of the sky and put it out before it explodes! Can you do it?'

Charlie nodded.

Josh lit the rocket. **WOOSH** – it took off towards the clouds. **WOOSH** – Charlie leapt up, chasing after it.

One . . . Two . . . Three . . . Charlie caught up with the rocket and reached out his hand, but suddenly the rocket violently changed direction and flew straight into his open mouth.

Four ... **KABOOM!**

Charlie flipped over backwards with multicoloured sparks shooting out of his ears and nostrils. 'Arghh ...' he plummeted back towards the ground and – **THUMP** – landed on the safety matting surrounding a children's playground.

Josh grimaced. 'Ouch, that's definitely gotta hurt.'

Charlie clutched his throat. 'Josh, quick, get me some water – I think my tongue is on fire!'

One hour and two ice blocks later, Charlie
returned home. But as he walked into the kitchen –
DING-DONG – the doorbell rang loudly.

Charlie rushed down the hallway to open the
door but – **KERSLAM** – it collapsed in front of
him. An old man puffing and wheezing waddled
over the top of it.

'Goodness gracious,' the old man marvelled.
'Sometimes I forget how strong I still am.'

'Grandpa!' Charlie cried.

'Charlie, my boy,' Grandpa said with a beaming
smile. 'Great to see you!'

Just then, Mum, Dad and Trixie rushed to greet
Grandpa.

'Oh, my word, Wallace – this is a most
unexpected visit,' said Mum. 'What are you doing
here? I thought we were going to visit you at your
new rest home during the school holidays.'

Grandpa shook his head. 'Oh, no, that's not
going to happen now. Not now that the blinkin'
rest home has sunk.'

'Sunk?' Mum said, staring at Grandpa. 'Your rest home has sunk? How did that happen?'

Grandpa dabbed his nose with his handkerchief. 'Well, you see, it was a cold, moonless night, and the sea was as flat as a pancake – it was a terrible night for spotting icebergs – a most dangerous night indeed for being out on the ocean. I told the captain to slow down, but he wanted to reach New York in record time . . .'

'Grandpa, stop, stop – that's not your story – that's the story of the sinking of the *Titanic*!' Charlie said.

Grandpa stopped mid-thought. 'By crikey, laddie, you know what? I think you're right. I thought that story sounded familiar.'

'Grandpa, tell us why you're not at your rest home any more.' Charlie said.

Grandpa dabbed his nose again. 'Ah, to tell you the truth, I couldn't stand the place – it was too boring and stuffy for me. All everyone wanted to do was sit around playing scrabble and talking about the good old days. No, that's not the life for me. I've still got plenty of adventures left in me. I'm too young to retire.' Grandpa puffed out his chest. 'I still want to serve the citizens of earth. I still want to be a superhero. I still want to make a difference. I still want to . . .'

Suddenly Grandpa leaned against the wall and his head flopped down. 'Zzzzzzzz . . .' he started snoring loudly.

'What's wrong with him?' asked Trixie.

'Um, I think Grandpa's having a little nap,' Charlie said.

After Grandpa awoke from his long nap, Mum revived him with a hot cup of tea and his favourite snack of all time – ginger nut biscuits.

'Wallace, I've just called the rest home,' Mum

said. 'I've told them you'll be staying with us for a while.'

'Fine by me,' Grandpa said, dunking his biscuit in his cup of tea. 'I'll be much safer here on dry land than being stuck out at sea amongst all those icebergs.'

Mum turned to Charlie. 'Ah, Charlie, Grandpa's going to need somewhere to sleep while he stays with us. I was wondering if he could have your room?'

'My room?' Charlie looked at Mum. 'But where am I going to sleep?'

'Ah, I thought, maybe you could move in with Trixie for a little bit?'

Charlie's jaw dropped. 'What? Me and Trixie share a room? No way, she'll never agree to that.'

Mum got up out of her chair. 'Don't worry, Charlie, I'll take care of it.'

She knocked on the living-room door. 'Trixie, Trixie darling, are you in there?'

Mum opened the door and did a double-take. Trixie was dancing in the middle of the living room like an out-of-control robot. Behind her,

on the TV, a recording of the previous night's *World's Greatest Pop Singer* was blaring at eardrum-shuttering levels.

'Trixie, you've been having sugary drinks again, haven't you?' Mum bellowed.

Trixie didn't respond. Her eyes were glazed over, zombie-like.

Charlie rushed in. 'What's happening?'

Mum groaned. 'I specifically told her not to have sugary drinks in the morning, and now look at her – she's as loopy as a lollipop.'

Charlie scratched his head and frowned. 'But

Mum, I don't get it, why's she still dancing like that? There's no music playing on the TV. There's just some short guy talking to three people.'

Charlie stopped and stared at the TV screen. 'Hey, wait a minute, that guy looks familiar . . .' But before he could take a closer look, Mum turned the TV off. She then grabbed Trixie's snaking left arm and carefully guided her back to the sofa.

'Now darling, I know you're not exactly feeling yourself right now, but I've got a huge favour I need to ask of you.'

Trixie bounced up and down on the sofa, frantically crossing and uncrossing her legs.

'Um, Grandpa's coming to stay with us for a while, and I need to know if it will be okay for you and Charlie to share a room together.'

Trixie sat completely still. She turned her head sideways and glared at Charlie.

Charlie covered his ears.

Trixie opened her mouth robotically. 'YESSSSSSS . . .'

THE POP SINGER FORMERLY KNOWN AS PANDEMONIUM

Sitting in his secret underground headquarters, the general grinned from ear to ear.

'I totally rocked the house last night, didn't I, Lieutenant?'

'Oh, yes you did, sir,' Lieutenant Kurse said, 'You rocked the house harder than a rocking horse rocking back and forth on a rocketing rocket.'

The general held up his wig and twirled it around the tip of his finger.

'And this wig certainly had everyone fooled. No one even slightly suspected that I was a supervillain in disguise. Hmmm, that was your idea to wear the wig, wasn't it, Lieutenant?'

Lieutenant Kurse nodded.

'Well, then, Lieutenant, I've just got one thing to say to you – for once in your life you didn't make a disastrous, earth-shatteringly stupid, decision.'

The Lieutenant's face lit up. 'Really, sir? Do you mean it? Oh my word, coming from you that's the highest of compliments!'

'So, Lieutenant, what gave you the idea for the disguise?'

'Well, sir, there's this new international singing sensation called Alannah Savannah who uses the same trick too. By day she's just a normal cowgirl living out on a farm – but by night, she puts on a blonde wig and – *violà!* – transforms herself into a mega-successful rock star with millions of adoring fans chasing after her.'

The general smiled. 'Ooh, I like the sound of that. I want to have a secret rock-star identity like Alannah Savannah does too.'

'Excuse me, sir? You want to be a cowgirl?'

'No, no, you numbskull, of course not.' The general puffed out his chest. 'By day I shall be the galaxy's most ruthless, merciless, bloodthirsty

supervillain – and by night I shall be a smokin'-hot
rock star with loads of crazy fans screaming out
my name and begging for my autograph. Ohh . . .
think about it, Lieutenant, the galaxy has never
seen a supervillain who's that seriously *cool* before!'

The general flipped the wig back on his head. 'All right, help me think of a snappy rock-star name like hers. Something that rhymes with Andy?'

Lieutenant Kurse thought for a moment. 'Oh, I know, sir. How about Andy Candy? Your name sounds sweet, but your music sounds even sweeter?'

'No, no, Lieutenant! Utterly hopeless. That name sounds like something you'd buy in a sweet shop.' The general smiled broadly. 'Ooh, I've got it, I've got the best name.' He stood up and struck a rock-star pose. 'How about this – everything goes grandly when you listen to *Andy Dandy*. Pretty groovy, eh? What do you think?'

The general nodded.

'Andy Dandy it is then, sir.'

The general preened his moustache. 'Okay, Lieutenant, I want Andy Dandy music videos, DVDs, mp3 downloads, ringtones, posters, calendars . . . the works!'

Lieutenant Kurse saluted the general. 'Right you are, sir.'

The general laughed loudly. 'Huh, move over

Alannah Savannah, you're old news; make way
for the coolest new pop singer in the world – Andy
Dandy!'

The intercom light flashed on the general's desk.

'General, we're ready for you in the command
centre,' Corporal Stench said.

The general took his wig off.

'Okay, Lieutenant, it's time to debrief the
dummies. Come on, follow me.'

He marched towards the door. 'Oh, and by the
way, Lieutenant, how come you know so much
about Alannah Savannah?'

Lieutenant Kurse blushed for a moment. 'U-um,
er, a *friend* told me about her, sir.'

THE BRAIN-BUSTING
BREAK-O-TRON

The general stood on a platform in front of his crew in the command centre.

'Men – I am proud to announce that phase one of my latest plan for world domination is successfully under way!'

'Hooray!' A cheer went up around the command centre.

'Owing to matters of extreme secrecy, and the fact that you are all a bunch of blabbering baboons, it is only now that I can reveal the full details of my plan to you.' The general snapped his fingers. 'Lieutenant, lights please.'

The background lights in the command centre dimmed and the image of a tall bearded man

appeared on the viewing screen.

'In the late 1970s, the brilliant evil French
scientist Pierre Le Boogie developed a way

to control people's minds and bodies using hypnotically laced disco dance music. In the early 1980s Pierre developed this a step further by using popular breakdancing music to create the world's most devastating mind-and-body controlling system called the Break-o-Tron.

'Sadly, before Pierre could unleash his weapon on the world, he was involved in a shocking mind-controlling experiment that went wrong and he was left in a permanent state of brain-dead breakdancing madness. Ever since Pierre's tragic accident, his weapon has remained hidden from the rest of the world.'

The general pulled a gold microphone out from behind his back.

'That is, until now.'

'Oohhhhh,' a hushed murmur rippled across the command centre.

The general tapped the end of the microphone. 'Prepare to see a live demonstration of my newly acquired weapon, the Break-o-Tron.'

WIRRR. A blast shield rose up to reveal a frail thin man standing nervously in a glass-panelled

34

soundproof room. The general stormed off the
platform and entered the glass-panelled room. He
clicked on his communicator and turned to his crew.

'Inside the microphone is a computer that
generates hypnotically laced breakdancing
music. When I sing into the microphone my
voice is mixed in with the music to produce a
mind-warping sound wave. Anyone
who hears this will
be temporarily
transformed into
a brain-dead
breakdancing zombie,
unable to resist my
commands. Let me
demonstrate . . .'

The general turned
off his communicator. He
raised the microphone to
his lips and began singing.
At once the frail thin man
began leaping about the
room uncontrollably. A few

seconds later the general stopped singing and left the room. He returned to the platform.

'I plan to use the Break-o-Tron to get people to vote me through to the grand final of *World's Greatest Pop Singer.* There, in front of the world's largest television audience, I will unveil phase two of my sinister plan.'

The general pulled out a platinum microphone from behind his back.

'Behold, Pierre Le Boogie's deadliest creation ever — the Break-o-Tron 2. It looks and sounds exactly the same as the original Break-o-Tron, but it has one major difference — its brainwashing effects are *permanent.*'

'Ooooo,' went another hushed murmur around the command centre.

The general preened his moustache. 'The effects of my first use of the Break-o-Tron lasted for only a few minutes, and were put down to some sort of mass hysteria rather than my genius. The fools suspected nothing! After I sing live in front of four billion or more people next month, I will transform the earth's population into a bunch of brain-dead

breakdancing zombies who will be forced to bop
until they drop. Muhaa-hhaa! And then, with
nearly every man, woman and child under my
control, I will take my rightful place as earth's new
leader! Muhaa-hhaa ...'

'Hooray!' A hearty cheer went up around the
command centre.

The general punched the air with his
microphone. 'That's all – crew dismissed,' he
said, walking away from the platform. Just then,
Corporal Stench approached him.

'Ah, sir, I think your plan is absolutely

incredible, perhaps your finest ever, but I have one question for you.'

The general swung round. 'What?'

'Sir, if nearly every human being is affected by the Break-o-Tron 2, won't it be extremely difficult trying to manage hordes and hordes of out-of-control zombies twenty-four hours a day, seven days a week?'

The general snarled at the corporal. 'Absolutely not. It'll be a piece of cake. In fact, I already have years and years of experience managing brain-dead zombies twenty-four hours a day, seven days a week.'

'Really, sir?' The corporal replied. 'Where on earth did you get that experience?'

The general folded his arms across his chest and frowned.

'Working here.'

DJ FREESTYLER FRISBY VS MC HIP HOP HEADMASTER

Three weeks later . . .

Charlie and Josh trudged down the hallway towards their classroom. Neither of them was looking forward to Mr Frisby's boring lesson about recycling.

'How are you going to stay awake during for the next hour?' Josh said.

Charlie reached into his bag. 'By reading this – it's Commander Ron's latest book *Fitter, Faster and More Fantastic*. It's the story of his childhood.' He opened the front page. 'Commander Ron even autographed it for me.'

'The world's greatest superhero autographed your book?' Josh said.

Charlie smiled. 'Sure . . .' He crossed two fingers together. 'Didn't you know that me and Commander Ron are like this nowadays.'

Charlie looked at Josh. 'What about you? How are you going to survive this torture test?'

Josh reached into his bag and pulled out his iPod. 'I've just downloaded an album by a new singer called Andy Dandy. It's meant to be the coolest album ever. Hopefully it will keep me sane until the bell goes.'

Josh and Charlie shuffled through the door and took their seats at the back of the classroom.

Mr Frisby stood at the front, furiously writing on the whiteboard.

Charlie carefully spread his book out and disguised it with his pencil case and a piece of paper. Josh, meanwhile, quietly slipped his earphones into his ears. He lifted up his iPod and went to press *play* but suddenly his fingers slipped and – **CLUNK** – he accidentally dropped the iPod in the middle of his desk.

'What was that?' Mr Frisby turned round from the whiteboard and glared.

Josh felt a lump in his throat. Charlie covered his eyes.

Mr Frisby strolled to the back of the classroom. Josh carefully slipped his iPod under his pencil case to hide it.

'Uh-hum,' Mr Frisby said, tapping him on the shoulder. 'Is my lesson not exciting enough for you this morning, Mr Eagle?'

'Ummmm . . . no,' Josh said pulling his earphones out. 'Er, recycling is a very exciting topic.'

Mr Frisby put his hand out. 'Okay, Mr Eagle, you know the rules about listening to music in my class, don't you?'

Josh nodded solemnly. He handed his iPod over to Mr Frisby.

'Need I remind you that this is a classroom, not a disco. If you want to get down and shake your booty, then I suggest you attend Mrs Silverston's after-school dance class. But while you're here, I would really appreciate it if you just sat quietly at your desk and didn't move a muscle, please.'

Mr Frisby stared at the iPod's menu. 'Andy Dandy? What sort of rubbish are you kids listening to these days?' He slipped the earphones into his ears and pushed *play*.

Suddenly his body jerked violently. His right arm shot out and wiggled up and down like a crawling caterpillar. His left arm shot out and started doing the same. Then his eyes glazed over,

zombie-like, and he moonwalked to the front of
the classroom, dropped down onto his head and
started spinning wildly in circles.

'Ha-hah-ha!' The class erupted with laughter.

'Wow, I never knew Mr Frisby was so athletic,'
commented Charlie.

KERTHUMP – Mr Frisby flopped back
down to the ground with his head resting on his
upturned elbow and his knee wrapped round the
back of his neck.

Just then Principal Wilson walked in. 'Excuse me, class, but has anyone seen Mr Frisby?'

'Ah, yes sir, he's over there by the computer table,' Josh informed him.

SWOOSH-SWOOSH – Mr Frisby suddenly slid across the front of the classroom arching up and down like a bouncing worm.

'Mr Frisby? My word, what's wrong with you?' Principal Wilson barked.

Charlie stood up. 'Sir, I think Josh's music is making him act crazy.'

Principal Wilson stomped his feet. 'What is Mr Frisby doing listening to music while he's teaching? Doesn't he know this is a classroom, not a disco!'

Charlie hopped out of his seat, ran to the front of the classroom and pulled the iPod off Mr Frisby.

'Sir, he can't help himself, I think the music is affecting his brain!' He held up the iPod.

SWOOSH-SWOOSH-SWOOSH – Mr Frisby continued snaking manically back and forth along the floor.

Principal Wilson snatched the iPod out of

Charlie's hands. 'What do you mean the music is affecting his brain? How ridiculous. I don't believe a word of what you're saying, lad.' He looked at the iPod then lifted the earphones towards his ears.

'No, don't do it!!!' Charlie bellowed.

But he was too late. Principal Wilson started jerking about violently. His right arm shot out and wiggled up and down through the air, followed by his left arm.

At that very moment Mr Frisby leapt to his feet and began gliding in circles around the

breakdancing principal.

'Hey, look – they're having a dance-off!' Josh cried out.

'Ha-ha-ha-ha!!!!' the class erupted again.

The door swung open and in raced Mrs Kurten from the classroom opposite. 'What's going on?' she howled, her eyes bulging.

'Um, miss, it appears that Mr Frisby and Principal Wilson are having a breakdancing competition,' Josh replied. 'I think Mr Frisby is winning.'

'What on earth . . . ?' Mrs Kurten clapped her hands. 'All right, everybody – leave the classroom immediately,' she boomed. 'Assemble in the courtyard and somebody call the school nurse to come and help!'

The children quickly evacuated the classroom. Charlie pulled Josh's iPod off Principal Wilson as he left the room. Josh turned round and took a photo of the two breakdancing teachers on his mobile phone.

'Good idea,' Charlie agreed. 'We can show that footage to the school nurse so she will know what's going on.'

'The school nurse?' Josh said, frowning. 'No way. I'm going to send these images to the makers of *The World's Wackiest Home Videos*. I've never seen anything so funny before in my life. It's bound to win me a prize.'

BiG, BAD AND BLiNGTASTiC

A short while later, much to their delight, Josh, Charlie and the rest of their class were sent home early from school.

'That's not how I thought our lesson on recycling would end,' Charlie said, looking at his watch.

'I know, I must bring my iPod along to more of Mr Frisby's lessons,' Josh chuckled.

Charlie lifted the iPod out of Josh's hands. 'So what's the deal with Andy Dandy's music? Why did it cause Mr Frisby and Mr Wilson to flip out so weirdly like that?'

Josh shook his head. 'I don't know. It was like they were under a spell. I heard that something similar happened when he sang on *World's Greatest Pop Singer* the other night. But I thought it was just a publicity stunt.' He grinned at Charlie. 'Hey, why don't you try listening to the song as well? Maybe your super powers will protect you from being brainwashed.'

Charlie handed the iPod back. 'Uh-uh. No way. I'm not taking any chances with that thing.'

Josh and Charlie passed a bus stop and headed towards the park. But when they crossed over the road – **WEE-ORR-WEE-ORR** – a police siren sounded in the distance.

'Charlie, what's up?' Josh cried, looking around.

Charlie concentrated hard with his super hearing. 'I think it's coming from the mall!'

'Okay, let's get going,' Josh urged.

Charlie sped off leaving a vapour trail behind him.

'Oi, wait up,' called Josh. 'We're not all built for super speed.'

Charlie slowed down. 'Oops, sorry.'

Two minutes later Josh and Charlie arrived at the mall. A police car with its lights flashing was parked in front of the cinema.

'What's going on?' asked Josh.

Charlie looked around. 'I don't know, I can't see anything obvious.' He glanced up at a huge poster hanging above the cinema's entrance. The poster showed a singer with an enormous nose and bright blond hair holding a golden microphone. Beneath the poster an electronic message flashed: 'See Andy Dandy's new music video on our big screen NOW!'

Charlie stopped and grabbed Josh's arm. His face went white.

'Charlie, what's wrong?' said Josh, alarmed.

Charlie pointed at the poster. 'Look at the nose! Don't you recognise it?'

Josh looked up.

'Josh, there's only one person in the galaxy who has a nose as enormous as that!' said Charlie. He took in a deep breath. 'General Pandemonium!'

Josh gasped and did a double-take. 'No way . . . It can't be. We got rid of him already, didn't we?'

Charlie shook his head. 'It's him all right, Josh. I'd never forget a nose like that. He pointed at the

See Andy Dandy's new video on our big screen NOW!!!

poster again. 'And check out the medallion he's wearing round his neck!'

Josh stared at the poster. He saw a shiny silvery poodle-shaped object hanging beneath Andy Dandy's collar.

'Poodle bling!' he exclaimed.

Charlie nodded. 'Remember when we last saw the general he had poodle-patterned undies? It's him, Josh, it's definitely him.'

Josh ran his hands through his hair. 'Oh this is

bad, Charlie; this is seriously bad. Andy Dandy is really General Pandemonium! That explains why everyone is acting so crazy when they hear his music. The general's up to something. He's messing with people's minds!'

Josh looked at his iPod. 'I'm *so* glad that I didn't listen to his song.'

'Not as glad as I am,' said Charlie.

'But I don't get it. How come no one has recognised he's the general?' Josh said. 'Surely that stupid blond wig hasn't got everyone else fooled, has it?'

Charlie shook his head. 'Think about it, Josh – no one else has seen him up close like we have. We're the only people on the planet who have been within two feet of that disgustingly huge bogey-filled schnozz.'

Josh frowned. 'Charlie, we've gotta stop him. We've gotta take him down before he starts warping more people's minds.'

'I know, but—'

Just then – WOOSH – three large muscular men in tights descended from the sky.

KERTHUMP – they
landed in front of Josh and
Charlie.

'Fear not, kids – we're
here to save the day,' the
first man said. 'I'm Marvo
Man and these are my
friends Thunder Tom and
Zappo.'

Charlie's face lit up.
'Marvo Man, Thunder
Tom and Zappo! How
cool. I have all of your
collector's cards at home.
Oh, by the way, let me
introduce myself, I'm a
superhero too, my name is
Hero Boy.'

Marvo Man brushed
past Charlie. 'Sorry,
son . . . I can't stop to
chat, I have work to do.'
He charged away towards

the theatre doors with Thunder Tom and Zappo in hot pursuit.

'Ah, Marvo Man, I wouldn't go in there if I were you,' Charlie warned. 'You might get brainwashed by the music that's playing!'

'Hah, I laugh in the face of danger, and I poke my tongue out at the risk of being brainwashed,' Marvo Man boomed, disappearing through the doors.

Charlie turned to Josh. 'Boy, I sure hope they're all prepared for what's about to happen.'

A few seconds later – KA-BOOM – Marvo Man, Thunder Tom and Zappo burst through a hole in the theatre's thick concrete wall. They flapped their hands then dropped to the ground and began belly-flopping across the car park, gouging out deep trenches behind him as they bounced along.

'Nup – they weren't prepared for that,' said Charlie.

Josh pulled out his mobile phone and started filming. 'I can't believe it – what are the odds of getting two classic entries for *The World's Wackiest*

Home Videos on the same day? I think these guys are even funnier breakdancers than Mr Frisby and Principal Wilson!'

Marvo Man, Thunder Tom and Zappo then dropped down onto their heads and started spinning around at supersonic speed. WIRRRRRRRR – they bored themselves straight into the ground and disappeared out of sight down three smoking holes.

Josh and Charlie rushed over to the holes and peered down.

Josh kept filming. 'Look at them go! At that speed they should hit the earth's core in about two minutes.'

Charlie rubbed his brow. 'They're legendary

superheroes all right, but they seriously need to work on their listening skills.'

REUARGHHHH! Suddenly a huge roar echoed behind Josh and Charlie. They turned round to see dozens of brain-dead moviegoers pouring out of the cinema.

'Oh, this is getting ridiculous!' Josh said. 'Look at them, the general's music has turned them all into breakdancing boneheads.'

Charlie shook his head in disbelief.

Just then, the electronic wording under the poster changed to: 'See Andy Dandy in the Live Final of *World's Greatest Pop Singer* on the Big Screen: Saturday Night'.

Josh pointed at the poster.

'Oh no . . . this could be disastrous. Do you know how many people watch that show? It's the most popular programme in history.' Josh put his hands on his hips. 'Just look how much chaos the general can cause when only a few people listen to his music. Imagine what will happen when nearly the entire planet tunes in to hear him sing.'

Charlie looked at the breakdancing zombies

and groaned loudly. 'Someone tell me this isn't happening!' He rocked his head back. 'Our teachers are going crazy, our superheroes are going crazy, and now General Pandemonium's back trying to make everyone else go crazy too! This is totally turning into one of the worst days ever . . .'

'Tell me about it,' Josh sighed. 'And to top it all off, I've just wasted 99p downloading a song that I'll never be able to listen to on my iPod.'

HAIL THE HYPER HAMSTER

SWISH-SWISH. The automated doors to General Pandemonium's office opened and Lieutenant Kurse walked in.

He stopped and saluted the general. 'Good morning, sir.'

General Pandemonium stared coldly at him. He slowly shook his head back and forth. 'No, Lieutenant – that's not the way you address me any more. Please use my new greeting.'

Lieutenant Kurse looked blankly at the general. 'Ah, your new greeting, sir?'

The general thumped his desk. 'Yes, Lieutenant, don't tell me you've forgotten it already? Don't you read your e-mails?'

'Sir?'

'From now on you are to greet me with "What's up, dog?" It's the way *cool* people speak to each other.' The general waved his hand. 'Okay, let's try it again.'

'Ah, er, okay, sir.' Lieutenant Kurse shuffled backwards out of the general's office. *SWISH-SWISH*. The doors opened and he backed through them. He waited a few moments in the hallway, then – *SWISH-SWISH* – re-entered the room.

He saluted the general. 'Um . . . what's up with your dog, sir?'

'No, no!!!' The general slammed his head on the desk.

'Er, sorry, I mean, what's your dog up to, sir? Oh, by the way, how is Mitty Wiffy?'

'Argh!!' The general's face turned blood red. He clenched his fist tightly and ground his teeth.

'Oh, forget it, Lieutenant. Honestly, teaching you to talk *cool* is like teaching a duck to roller skate.'

'Sir?'

The general took in a short deep breath. 'Okay,

Lieutenant, why are you here? Why are you interrupting me?'

Lieutenant Kurse pulled out a roll of magazines from behind his back. 'Sir, I have a little surprise for you ...'

The general looked up 'What?'

The lieutenant placed the magazines on the general's desk. 'Sir, you've made the cover of every magazine on sale today! Isn't it incredible?'

'Really?' The general rifled through the magazines, purring like a cat.

'Oh, look ... I'm on the cover of *Rock 'n' Roll Weekly*, *Showbiz Monthly*, the *World Reporter* ... and, and ... *Celebrity Poodle*!' The general held up the magazine.

'Hey, there's me and Miffy Wiffy on the cover wearing our matching cardigans.' The general bent down and kissed the magazine. 'Oh, hoo-da-cuty-wooty-wittle-little-diddle Miffy Wiffy-kins. Isn't she the cutest pet ever?'

The lieutenant awkwardly avoided staring at the general. 'A-hem,' he coughed distractingly. 'Now, sir, I also have another piece of

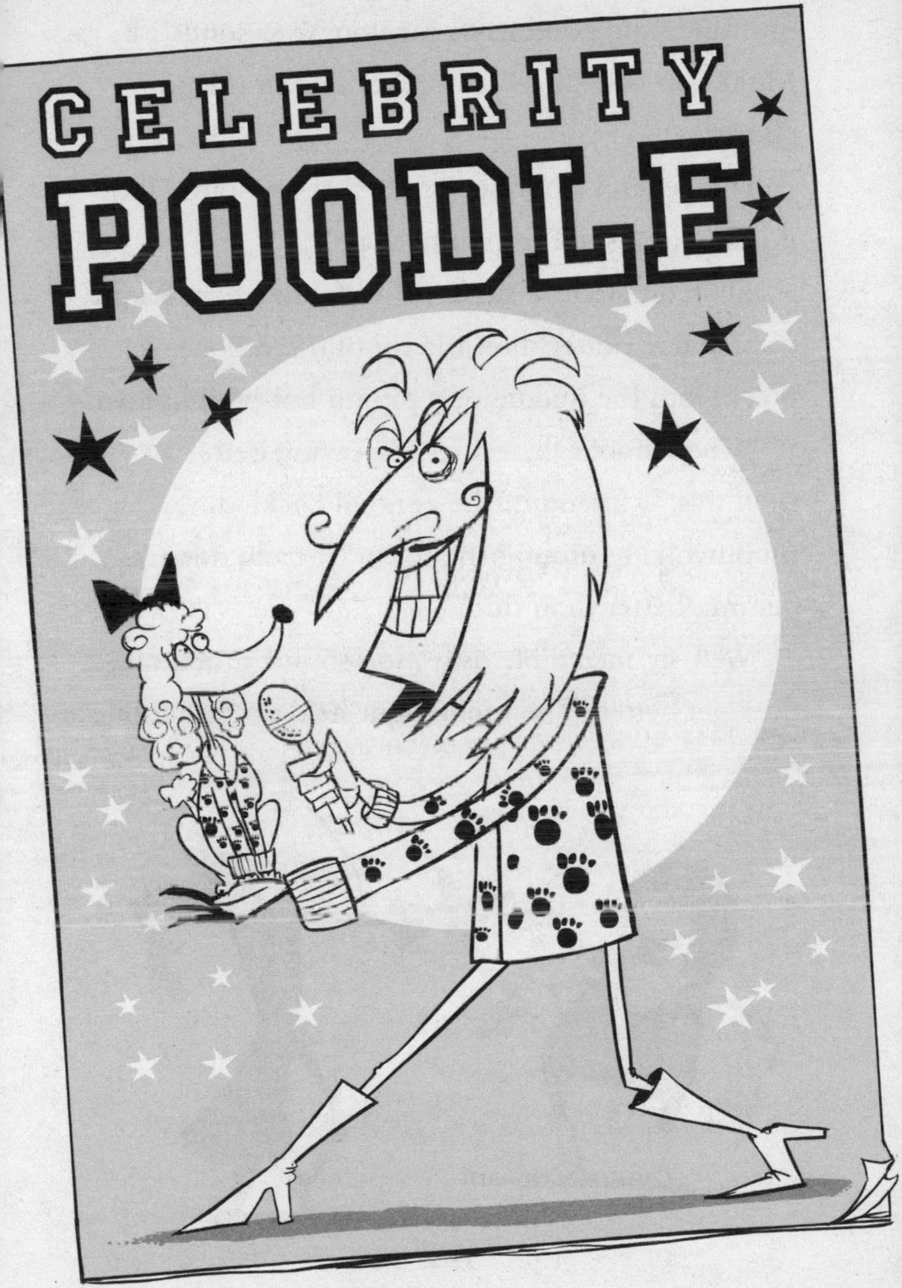
CELEBRITY
POODLE

outstandingly good news for you. Your song "I'll Make You My Slave" is number one in the pop charts!'

The general leapt out of his seat and did a little jig. 'Did you say I'm number one!'

Lieutenant Kurse smiled. 'I did indeed, sir. Right now, you're hotter than the tip of a red hot poker poked into the middle of a piping hot pool of lava.'

'Whoo-hoo! Oh, it doesn't get any better than this, Lieutenant,' the general cackled, moonwalking around the room. 'It truly doesn't get any better than this.'

'Well, sir, incredible as it may sound, it actually does get better!' The Lieutenant held up his mobile

phone. 'Just one hour ago I received a text from a producer at Whopper Records. Sir, they want you to record a duet with Hyper Hamster tomorrow morning!'

The general stopped moonwalking. He stared at the lieutenant. 'Hyper who?'

'Hyper Hamster, the most famous hamster on the planet. Surely you know his catchy ringtone, don't you – Bing-Bing-Bing Bong-Bing-Bing Bong?'

A blank look appeared on the general's face.

'Um, he's the biggest selling animal artist in history. He's won four World Music Awards and holds the record for the most downloaded ringtone of all time!'

The general put his hands on his hips. 'Lieutenant, I liked the first bit of news you gave me, but I find this second bit extremely disturbing. Do you honestly expect me to sing a duet with a hamster?'

Lieutenant Kurse raised his hand. 'Sir, before you decide, I need to let you know that Whopper Records plan to release the song as a digital charity single to raise funds for world peace. Sir, you know what this means, don't you? The song will be played on *every* radio station in *every* single country in the world. Think of the publicity you'll get – everyone will love you!'

The general said nothing.

'Sir, it's also a known fact that if you're asked to record a song with Hyper Hamster then you're cooler than ice.'

The general sat down and groaned. 'Honestly, agreeing to do something like this would go against everything I believe in. A duet with a stupid hamster? Hah! And as for world peace – eughh, the very thought of world peace makes me sick to my stomach.' He rolled his eyes. 'But . . . I'll do it because I want to be fantastically popular and world famous.'

The general got up, shook his head and walked towards the door. 'Now, Lieutenant, just because I'm agreeing to sing a duet with a hamster, this doesn't mean I want you or the men starting to think I'm going soft, okay?'

'No, sir, we wouldn't dare dream of it.'

SWISH-SWISH. The doors opened in front of the general.

'Ah, sir – where are you heading to now?' enquired the lieutenant.

The general walked through. 'I'm off to have a facial and get my nails done,' he shouted over his shoulder. 'I want to make sure I'm looking my best for the grand final.'

THE SUPER SILLY SUPER SECRET

Three days later . . .

DING-DONG. The Applejacks' doorbell rang loudly again. Charlie quickly raced down the stairs and opened it.

'Are you ready to save the world again?' Josh boomed. He held up a hand-drawn plan of the city. 'The general's attending a celebrity afternoon tea at the Spiral Tower at half-past four to celebrate Hyper Hamster's fifth birthday. We can nab him there before he makes it to the final.'

Charlie gave Josh the thumbs up. 'Sounds good to me.' He slipped his goggles over his eyes, 'Okay, let's do it!'

Just then Mum tapped him on the shoulder.

'Ah, Charlie, I heard that you and Josh are going on a little outing today. Would you mind taking Grandpa along with you? I'm sure he'd love to come.'

'Take Grandpa . . . ?'

'Yes, he's been dying to get out of the house, and I think we could all do with a break from his round-the-clock bagpiping and yodel-gargling too.'

'But Mum, this isn't just some *little* outing we're going on – we're going on a mission to save the world!'

'Yes, dear, I know you are,' Mum said. 'And it's very good of you to help out; but I think it's also important that you spend some quality time with your grandfather.'

Before Charlie could respond, Grandpa came barrelling down the hallway dressed in what looked like an old pair of pyjamas with the giant letters 'WW' sewn on the front. 'Wonder Wally to the rescue,' he bellowed, thrusting out his arm and charging towards the door.

Mum stared into Charlie's eyes. 'Please? He's been looking forward to this all morning.'

Charlie groaned. 'Um . . . okay . . . but only if I *really* have to.'

'Thanks, dear,' Mum said.

Charlie turned and bolted out the door. He joined Josh and Grandpa on the lawn.

'Okay, so what's our mission today?' said Grandpa, rubbing his hands together. 'Are we going to rescue a cat stuck up a tree or save a bridge from collapsing?'

'Ah, Grandpa, we're actually on a mission to save the world,' Charlie said.

Grandpa puffed out his chest. 'By jingo, that sounds like my sort of thing. Count me in!' He punched the air with his fist. 'So who's the baddy in this rumble?'

'General Pandemonium,' Charlie answered.

'General Pandemonium, eh? I can't say I've heard of him. 'Okay, then tell me, who are the goodies?'

Charlie and Josh glared at Grandpa. 'We are!!' they said in unison.

'Oh, great, great,' Grandpa said. 'That's much better. I always prefer playing for the goodies' team.'

Josh looked at his watch. 'Okay, we'd better get moving, there's no time to spare.'

Charlie looked round. 'Right, but first we need to find some transport.'

Josh frowned. 'Charlie, you really need to spend more time thinking about transport issues if you want to save the world on a regular basis.'

'Transport? Did someone say transport?'
Grandpa said. 'Don't worry, leave it to me, I've
got transport covered.' He waddled off towards the
garage.

Charlie looked at Josh.

TOOT-TOOT! A few seconds later he
returned riding a bright red mobility scooter.

Josh scratched his head.

'Ah, Grandpa, I'm not sure that's exactly what

we had in mind,' Charlie said.

'Heh-heh, fear not, laddie, I've had some snazzy new bells and whistles added.' Grandpa flipped a switch and – **FZZOAR** – the scooter slowly hovered off the ground and floated in mid air.

'Cool,' Josh said, smiling.

'All aboard, landlubbers; this ship is about to set sail.'

Josh and Charlie jumped on the back of Grandpa's scooter. **WIRRRRR** – they gradually floated up into the sky.

'Hey, Charlie, your grandpa is sure full of surprises isn't he?' Josh said, watching the ground disappear below him. He turned to Charlie, but Charlie didn't respond. He just stood frozen to the spot.

A tiny black spider crawled up the back of Grandpa's seat in front of him.

'S-s-spider!!' Charlie wailed. 'S-s-spider!!!'

Josh stared at the spider. 'What? Charlie, you can't be serious? Are you scared of that little spider on Grandpa's back?'

Charlie nodded. 'G-get rid of it.'

Grandpa turned round. 'What's all the fuss about back there?'

'Grandpa, I think Charlie's scared of that spider on your shoulder.'

Grandpa reached round and scooped the spider up. 'What, he's scared of this little cutie? No way.' Grandpa waved the spider in front of Charlie's face. 'Look, he's friendly.'

'Arghh,' Charlie sank to his knees, quivering and shaking.

'Ah, Grandpa, I think you really should get rid of the spider,' Josh pleaded.

'Okey-dokey.' Grandpa flicked the spider over

the side of the scooter. 'Fly, be free, little fella, use your cobwebby parachute to save yourself.' Grandpa looked down into the Applejacks' garden. 'Oops, I don't think he opened his parachute.'

Charlie stood back up.

'Charlie, you never told me you were scared of spiders,' Josh said.

'Um, well, it's not exactly the sort of thing a superhero likes to advertise, if you know what I mean.'

'Don't worry, lad, I used to be scared of spiders too,' Grandpa chuckled. 'Then I started nursery school . . . ha-ha-ha-ha.'

Charlie turned beetroot red. 'Listen, I'd really appreciate it if everyone kept this little secret to themselves. The world doesn't need to know I'm scared of spiders.'

Charlie tapped Grandpa on the shoulder.

'Hey, what about you, Grandpa? Surely you have some embarrassing secret weakness that you'd prefer nobody else knew about?'

Grandpa laughed. 'Nup, nothing wacky like that.' He pursed his lips. 'Oh, hang on a tick, well there is this one little humdinger.'

'What?'

'I have a terrible secret weakness.'

'What is it?' asked Charlie.

'I have absolutely no ability to keep secrets. Never have been able to, never will be able to. My mother used to call me Blabber Boy when I was a kid.'

Charlie's face dropped. 'Oh, that's just great, Grandpa. Now you've really made my day.'

Josh tapped his watch. 'Okay, guys, let's cut the chatter and get back to saving the world!'

'All righty then,' Grandpa bellowed, tooting his horn again.

VROOM – he revved the scooter's engine hard. 'World, watch out, we're coming to save you!' he yodelled. But suddenly he took his foot off the accelerator and floated the scooter back down to the ground. He jumped off and ran towards the house.

'Grandpa, what's wrong?' Charlie cried. 'Have you forgotten something?'

'Sorry – I've desperately gotta pee!' Grandpa said. 'At my age, when I've gotta go, I've *really* gotta go! Saving the world will have to wait five minutes.'

10

SAYONARA, ALANNAH SAVANNAH

The general's limousine pulled in for a brief stop at the Spiral Tower on its way to the *World's Greatest Pop Singer* live grand final at the Mega Dome.

'Now, Lieutenant, I want to make this clear from the start: I will absolutely not be singing "Happy Birthday" to Hyper Hamster, do you understand?'

'Loud and clear, sir.'

'Nor will I be playing pin the tail on the donkey, or pass the parcel, or any other such stupid game.'

'Roger that, sir. Er, how about the lolly scramble, sir?'

The general paused for a moment. 'Hmm, it

depends . . . if they're giving away Super Squishy Choco Nuggets then maybe I could be talked into it.'

BING. Lieutenant Kurse looked down at his laptop. A new e-mail had arrived.

'Oh, sir, good news. The latest Teen Popularity Charts have just come in. We'll be able to see exactly how much people love you.' The lieutenant clicked the screen but suddenly his face dropped.

The general looked concerned. 'Give it to me.' He snatched the computer out of the lieutenant's hands.

He looked at the screen and roared with disapproval.

'Most popular pop singer, Alannah Savannah! Coolest rock video, Alannah Savannah! Best hair, Alannah Savannah! Lieutenant, this is outrageous. No one beats me to number one! It's my right to be number one.'

'Sir, perhaps those figures aren't accurate. Computers have been known to make mistakes before.'

The general frowned. 'I will not tolerate this, Lieutenant. I will not allow some puffed-up ponytailed little princess to outperform me.' He cracked his knuckles.

'I'm going to have Alannah Savannah vaporised this instant!'

Lieutenant Kurse's jaw dropped. 'Sir, surely you can't be serious? I'll be . . . I mean, her fans will be devastated, sir. Isn't that excessively ruthless and cold-hearted, even by your own ruthless and cold-hearted standards?'

The general shrugged his shoulders. 'Hey, Lieutenant, this is showbusiness! People kill to get ahead all of the time!'

The general folded his hands behind his head

77

and sat back.

'Driver!' he boomed, rapping his knuckles on the plastic panel. 'I've changed my mind. Forget this stupid birthday party. Put your foot down and get a move on, I've got a planet to take over and I don't want to be held up by traffic jams.'

11

WHERE'S WONDER WALLY?

Twenty minutes later . . .

Charlie, Josh and Grandpa descended from the
clouds above the centre of the city.

Josh looked at his watch. 'Man that took way
longer than I thought it would. I can't believe how
slow your Grandpa's super scooter is. I think it
would have been faster walking.'

Charlie looked at Josh. 'I think Grandpa's
scooter is built more for comfort than speed.'

'Plus Grandpa stopping to go to the toilet
six times didn't help either,' Josh added. 'I think
he should change his superhero name to "The
Fountain".'

He looked down at the Spiral Tower below him. 'We're too late to arrest the general at the birthday party now!'

'Okay, where else could we find him?' Charlie said.

Josh pulled out his map. 'The grand final's at six o'clock at the Mega Dome, but right now he could be anywhere in the city.'

Charlie groaned. 'We've gotta find him, Josh, we've gotta stop him before he gets anywhere near the final.' He tapped Grandpa on the shoulder. 'Take us over the centre of town, Grandpa!' Charlie peered over the side of the scooter. 'I'm going to super scan every piece of the city I can and try to find him. But it won't be easy – he's

probably hidden himself right away.'

Josh looked directly behind the scooter and pointed furiously. A long black stretch limousine sped past below them with a flashing neon sign saying *Andy Dandy* on its roof.

Charlie pursed his lips. 'Okay, so that wasn't as difficult as I thought it would be.'

He tapped Grandpa on the shoulder. 'Grandpa, fly over to that crossroads on the left and land behind that big white concrete mixer next to the roadworks.'

'Okey-dokey.' Grandpa steered the scooter through the air and landed behind the concrete mixer.

Charlie, Josh and Grandpa jumped off the scooter.

'All right, action stations,' Charlie yelled.

'Okay . . .' Grandpa ran down the street. 'Who wants fries with their burger?'

Charlie waved him back. 'Grandpa, what are you doing? We're not stopping for lunch, we're saving the world, remember?'

'Oh yeah, right, right' Grandpa hummed, trundling back. 'Come on, then, let's quickly save the world and *then* eat – I'm starving!'

Charlie pointed at the general's limousine that was heading towards them in the distance. 'Okay, this is going to be a three-man surprise attack. Josh, you get the limousine to stop. Grandpa, you jump inside and grab the steering wheel, and then I'll roll under the limousine and lift it off the ground.'

Grandpa wiped his nose again. 'And then we eat?'

'Grandpa!' Charlie barked.

'Quick, look, he's coming!' shouted Josh.

The long black limousine turned right at the crossroads and travelled down the street towards the concrete mixer.

Josh ran out into the road, waving his arms.
'Andy, Andy, stop I want your autograph please.'

The limousine screeched to a halt. A dark-tinted
window slid down. Josh thrust his hand through it.
'Andy, Andy, you're the greatest singer ever   can
you autograph my arm, please?'

The general glared at Josh. 'Hey, wait a minute,
I recognise you – you're that big-mouthed little
friend of Zero Boy, aren't you?'

'What do you mean, Andy? I'm your biggest
fan!'

Just then Grandpa flung the passenger door
wide open and leapt in next to the driver. 'Freeze,
mister – reach for the stars!' he bellowed.

'Huh?' the driver said.

Suddenly – **SWOOSH** – Charlie rolled under
the car and – **HUMPHH** – stood up and lifted it
high above his head.

'Gotcha now, General!' Charlie boomed.

Josh, grinning, pointed his finger upwards. 'Hah
– you lose . . . *again*, big nose!'

The general leaned from the window and
glared at Josh. 'Let me guess, it's your annoying

little shower-curtain-wearing friend underneath our car right now, isn't it?'

Josh looked at Charlie. 'Okay, Charlie, now what?' he whispered.

Charlie grunted. 'Police! I'll take them to the nearest police station . . .' Charlie struggled forward awkwardly, gasping for breath. 'Josh, I can't exactly see where I'm going right now, can you guide me there?'

'Sure.' Josh sprinted to the other side of the road.

'Okay, walk forward about ten metres and then swing left.'

Charlie lumbered forward, but mistakenly swung right.

'No! Charlie, watch out for the . . .'

KERCLUNK – Charlie disappeared down a hole.

' . . . roadworks!'

The limousine thumped back down on to the road and – **SCREECH** – sped off into the distance.

Josh ran across the road. 'Charlie, are you okay?' He stared down into the muddy hole.

'Arghh . . .' Charlie groaned loudly.

'Charlie, what's wrong? Have you broken something?'

'No, worse,' Charlie said. 'My swimming cap fell off and I've got some chewing gum stuck in my hair! **EUGHH** – the stuff just won't come out.' He lifted his foot up. 'Ugh, and now there's some stuck to my shoe as well! It's disgusting. I can't walk properly.'

WHOOSH – Charlie jumped back up onto the street. 'That was *so* revolting down there . . . I never want to do that again.' He looked around. 'Hey where's Grandpa?'

Josh frowned. 'He's gone. He was in the limo – the general's got him!'

Charlie pulled his shoe off and tried to scrape away the gum. 'Okay, so that plan didn't exactly work out the way we intended.'

'What are we going to do now?' Josh said.

Charlie looked at Josh. 'Let's switch to Plan B.'

'Plan B? What's Plan B?' asked Josh.

Charlie wiped his brow. 'I'm not sure. But give me a minute and I'll try to think of it.'

THE TERRIBLE TALE OF THE TRUTH-TELLING TORTURE

Speeding towards the Mega Dome, General Pandemonium poked a laser blaster into the back of Grandpa's neck.

'Okay, old man, talk ... who are you and how on earth did you get here?'

'Well, my name is Wallace Trevorian Humperdinck Applejack the Third ...' Grandpa coughed loudly. 'And, let me see ... it all began a very long time ago. First, my mother and father met at a crossword-puzzle tournament, fell in love, got married and tried to adopt an albino tree frog as their child. However, after that didn't work out, they decided to have me instead ...'

'No, no, you crusty old coot, I don't want to know your personal history. I mean where did you come from just now?'

'The sky.'

'The sky? What were you doing in the sky?'

'Flying . . .'

'Flying? Why were you flying?' the general barked.

'Because sailing's just too bloomin' dangerous these days. You try sailing out on the ocean and then slamming into one of those gigantic icebergs and see who comes off best. No, no, my sailing days are well and truly over now.'

The general groaned and gnashed his teeth. 'Silence!' He released the safety catch on the laser blaster. 'Prepare to be vaporised, you annoyingly stupid old goon!'

'No, no, sir, don't do it . . .' Lieutenant Kurse said, placing his hand on the laser blaster. 'Sir, the old man might know something about Zero Boy that we don't.'

'Hah, why should I care about that snotty-nosed little twerp? What does he matter to me?'

'Sir, I don't want to dwell on negatives, but you do remember that last time he thwarted your plans to take over the world, don't you? Sir, he doesn't seem to have any weaknesses that we can exploit. Not even our Moozem affects him.'

The general sneered. 'Hah, he didn't stop me taking over the world last time. I just didn't feel like doing it that day. I had a headache.'

Lieutenant Kurse rustled about in his briefcase. He pulled out a giant syringe filled with a purple-coloured solution. 'Sir – I think this might be a golden opportunity to find out if Zero Boy has a secret weakness or not. I can inject the old man with vexotyde to force him to tell us everything he knows.'

The general frowned and glared at the lieutenant.

'Sir . . . please? It won't take a moment.'

The general sighed. 'Oh, all right, then, but only if you promise to stop nagging me.'

The general glared at Grandpa. 'Okay, old man – you've got one chance to tell us if the superkid has a secret weakness or not.'

Lieutenant Kurse held the syringe up in front of
Grandpa.

'And if you don't, we'll inject you with the
world's most powerful truth serum and you'll be
forced to tell us anyway.' The general rubbed his
hands together. 'But I must warn you, one dose of
vexotyde will make your fingers swell to the size
of hotdogs and leave your eyeballs feeling like
boiling billiard balls.'

Grandpa turned to the general. 'Wait – don't do
it, you're wasting your time; your vexotyde won't

have any effect on me!'

The general snarled. 'Oh, so you want to play the tough guy now, do you? Is our puny truth serum is too weak and wimpy for your big muscular body?'

Grandpa shook his head. 'No, no, you don't understand, I have absolutely no ability to keep secrets. It's pointless torturing me. Listen, I'll tell you everything you want to know about the boy . . .'

The general looked at the lieutenant and laughed. He turned back to Grandpa. 'Very well, old man, tell us what his secret weakness is.'

Grandpa drew a deep breath, '*Spiders!* The boy's dead scared of spiders! They make him cry like a little baby. That's his secret weakness.'

The general's eyes blazed. 'What? How ridiculous! Don't lie to me! Do you honestly expect me to believe that a superhero is scared of spiders? Hah, no way.'

He turned to the lieutenant.

'Go ahead, inject him with vexotyde, and double the dosage. I want to see this old geezer in unimaginable mind-numbing pain!'

The lieutenant squirted the syringe in front of Grandpa's face.

Grandpa turned sheet white. 'Argh!! No . . .'

BOLD, BRAVE AND BULGING

HUMPHH. Charlie kicked out his back legs, propelling the wobbling super scooter through the sky.

'Hey, Charlie, can you try to power us more smoothly?' Josh said, hanging on for dear life to the scooter's handlebars. I'm feeling air sick.'

'Sorry!' Charlie boomed. 'I'm still trying to get the hang of this flying business.'

A few minutes later Charlie and Josh were soaring shakily above the Mega Dome.

'Hey, look, there's the general's car, he beat us here already,' Josh observed.

'Okay, take us down,' ordered Charlie.

Josh tilted the handlebars forward and dropped the scooter's nose into a steep dive. But suddenly the machine began to plummet uncontrollably towards the ground.

'Hit the brakes, Josh!' Charlie hollered.

Josh desperately searched the controls. 'Brakes? Charlie, I don't think this thing has brakes!'

Charlie looked down and screamed loudly 'Arghh!!!' But as his mouth opened wide the whipping wind rushed in and – **WiRAPPPP** – inflated his body to the size of a hot-air balloon.

He gripped the scooter tightly and helped it float safely towards the ground. *KERRUMP*. A few moments later Charlie and Josh landed gently in the middle of the Mega Dome's car park.

Charlie stood up and – **BAAARRRP** – let out an enormous super belch, deflating his body back to its normal size.

BAAARRP!

Josh gave him a high five. 'Charlie, I didn't know you were inflatable. How seriously cool! Hey, can I borrow you next weekend? I promised Mum we'd take her on a hot-air balloon ride for her birthday!'

Charlie frowned and **PHEEPP** – let out a final gust of air. He looked at his watch. 'Okay, the general's going to be singing any minute now – c'mon, let's go.'

Josh and Charlie ran across the car park and headed towards the main entrance of the Mega Dome. A guard moved to stop them but they rushed straight past him and darted into the lobby.

'Okay, what now? Where's the general?' Josh cried.

Suddenly a large triangular shadow appeared around a corner of a wall.

'It's the general!' Charlie shouted. Josh and Charlie dived for cover behind a large sofa. A few seconds later the general and Lieutenant Kurse walked briskly into the lobby. They stopped in front of the sofa.

The lieutenant held up the Break-o-Tron 2 microphone. 'Okay, sir, the microphone is fully tested and ready for use. It will hypnotise the audience as soon as you start singing; if you continue for sixty seconds, this purple light will start flashing and then the brainwashing effects will become permanent and irreversible.'

The general snatched the microphone out of the lieutenant's hands.

Josh nudged Charlie. 'Do something . . .'

Charlie looked at Josh. 'How many henchmen are with the general?'

Josh peered around the sofa. 'Um, just one. He's

wearing . . . I think . . . is that Alannah Savannah
cowboy boots?'

Charlie gritted his teeth. 'Okay, Josh, on the
count of three, you distract the goon and I'll tackle
the general and destroy his microphone.'

Josh nervously nodded.

'Okay, one, two . . .' But suddenly Charlie put
his hand up. He clutched his ear. His super hearing
had detected a desperate cry for help.

He turned to Josh. 'It's Grandpa. I think he's in
danger!'

14

THE ATTACK OF THE SERIOUSLY SMALL SPIDER

The general stormed away from the sofa towards the theatre.

'Look – the general's getting away!' Josh cried.

'I know,' Charlie howled. 'But we've gotta save Grandpa first.' He grabbed Josh's arm and pulled him away from the sofa. The two boys then sprinted down a long hallway. Charlie concentrated hard with his super hearing. 'He's around here somewhere.' He led Josh around a corner then stopped dead in front of a door marked 'Staff Only'.

'Help me, help me,' a frail voice called from behind the door.

'Grandpa, what's happening?' Charlie boomed. 'Is someone hurting you? Is your life in danger?'

'No,' Grandpa barked. 'I'm locked in the blinkin' toilet and I can't get out!'

HARGGHH – Charlie smashed the door down. Lying on the ground in front of him was Grandpa, moaning and groaning.

'Grandpa!' Charlie wailed. 'Who did this to you? And what's happened to your fingers? They're huge!'

Grandpa rolled over. 'Oh, some nasty beggar wearing rodeo boots gave me an injection with a dirty great needle. It made my fingers swell to the size of hotdogs and gave me a headache the size of Texas. The pain isn't the worst thing, though – I'm as hungry as a horse and sitting here staring at my fingers is just about doing my head in.'

'Can you walk, Grandpa?'

'Nup, I'm as dizzy as a goose.'

Charlie picked Grandpa up and threw him over his shoulder. 'C'mon, Grandpa, we can't wait any longer, we've got to stop the general before he brainwashes the world!'

Charlie bounded out into the hallway.

'Wait . . . wait . . .' demanded Grandpa, tapping him on the back. 'Take me back – take me back in there.'

'What? Take you back? We've just rescued you.'

Grandpa's face was strained. 'No, I think I need to go to the loo again!'

Charlie groaned. 'Grandpa – what are you? A human leaky tap? No, you'll just have to hold on until after we save the world.'

Charlie turned and bounded down the hallway with Josh sprinting behind, trying his best to keep up. A few moments later they made it back to the lobby.

Josh reached into his pocket and handed the earplugs his mum had given him when he'd told her he was going to the final of *World's Greatest Pop Star*. 'Okay, everybody, put these in now so you won't get brainwashed by the general's music.'

Charlie squished the earplugs and folded them into his ears. Grandpa licked his lips and popped them straight into his mouth. 'Mmmm, minty . . .,' he said, swallowing them whole.

'No, Grandpa, you're not meant to eat them, you put them in your ears!' Josh told him.

He looked at Charlie. 'What do we do with Grandpa? That was the last pair. If he listens to the general singing, he might lose his mind.'

Charlie arched his eyebrows. 'Josh, I think we're way past worrying about that.'

Charlie turned and headed towards the theatre entrance. 'C'mon, follow me.'

The intrepid threesome quietly slipped in unnoticed to the back of the darkened theatre. At the front of the stage, under the spotlight, the general was talking with the judges.

Damon Scowl leaned into his microphone and sneered. 'You know what, Andy, I genuinely think you deserve to be up there on the stage today.'

The general looked surprised. 'Really?' he muttered in a low voice.

'Yes, Andy. And, do you know what you should be doing on the stage?'

The general shook his head.

'Sweeping it!'

'Ha-ha-ha-ha!' The audience erupted with

laughter. The general clenched his fist angrily.

Cindy Fizzwick leaned across Damon Scowl. 'Oh, don't listen to him, Andy, he's just jealous of your fab hair.' Cindy smiled at the general. 'Now tell us, Andy, do you think you have what it takes to blow our minds in the final?'

The general grinned. 'Yes, Cindy. What I'm holding here in my hands will absolutely guarantee that!'

Just then Charlie charged down the aisle and – **BOINGG** – flew up onto the stage.

'Ohhhhhhh . . .' A shocked hush fell across the audience.

Charlie stood in front of the judges and pointed his finger angrily at the general. 'Everybody, listen to me. This creep is not who you think he is! He's not a pop singer – he's really a talentless evil scumbag pretending to be a pop singer.'

Damon Scowl stood up and applauded. 'Finally, we're getting some honesty around this place. Son, would you like to join us on the judging panel?'

Charlie glared at the general. 'All right, General, the game's finished. Give yourself up now. I've

beaten you again.'

The general half-smiled. 'I'm sorry, son, I really
don't know what you're talking about. I think you
have me mistaken for somebody else.'

Charlie puffed out his chest. 'Don't play games
with me, General – you've sung your last song.
This party's over!'

Charlie raised his fists and moved towards the
general. But the general quickly reached into his
pocket and pulled out a tiny object. He put his
hand up in front of Charlie's face.

'I wouldn't get any closer if I were you,' he

laughed. 'Especially not when you see what I'm holding in my hand.'

The general opened his fist to reveal a hairy spider sitting in the middle of his palm.

Charlie froze with fear, then dropped to his knees. 'ARGGHH Spider! Spider! A h-hairy disgusting s-spider!' He fell to the floor and curled up into a ball, whimpering and sobbing. The television cameras zoomed in on his poor helpless form.

Josh covered his eyes. 'Oh no, I think Charlie's

embarrassing secret has just gone totally global.'

The general then turned to the audience.

'Sorry about that interruption, folks, but like they say, the show must go on.' He struck a cool rock star pose. 'All right, everybody, prepare to bop until you drop!'

BOY ZERO -
BREAKDANCING HERO

The general clicked a button at the base of his microphone and held it up to his lips. **BOOM-DUM-DUM-DA-BOOM**. The studio echoed with a thumping bass sound and the general blasted out the first notes of his song. Immediately the entire audience rose from their seats and began breakdancing uncontrollably.

Grandpa leapt to his feet and started manically back-flipping.

The video screens adorning the walls beamed images of people wildly breakdancing all across the world.

Josh clasped his head in his hands, watching the general sing. 'NOOOO!! This isn't happening!' Suddenly – **BUMPFF** – an out-of-control

brain-dead breakdancing zombie accidentally knocked him off his feet.

He picked himself up and crawled along the carpet, then climbed onto the stage. He ran over to Charlie's twitching body. 'Charlie, Charlie, snap out of it. For goodness' sake snap out of it!' he pleaded, shaking his quivering friend. But Charlie was locked in his own spider-scared world.

Josh glanced over at the general, then back at Charlie.

'Charlie, please . . . forgive me for doing this!' He bent down and pulled the earplugs out of Charlie's ears.

Charlie immediately leapt to his feet and began breakdancing with a zombie-like expression on his face. His arms flapped up and down and – **WOOSH** – he launched himself into the air like a helicopter. **KERASHH** – he smashed into the top of the theatre's roof and – **KERSLAM** – crashed back to the ground again.

'What the . . . ?' The general turned round and looked to his left.

While he was distracted Josh quickly ran up

behind him and ripped the microphone out of his hands. He ran over to Charlie.

'Hero Boy . . . Freeze!' Josh bellowed through the microphone.

Charlie rose up and froze like a statue.

'Hero Boy . . . you are not scared of spiders any more! They are your friends!'

Charlie's mouth dropped wide open. 'Hero Boy is not afraid of spiders any more.'

He bent down and patted the spider on its head. 'Hello, you are my friend. Do you want to dance?'

Josh turned and pointed at the general. 'Hero Boy, stop the general and save the world!'

Charlie sprung back up and moonwalked across to the general. He lifted him up in the air,

spun him around in circles then – **KERBASH** –
slammed him head-first into the stage.

'Owfff,' Josh said, grimacing. 'Now that's what I
call *break* dancing!'

Charlie moonwalked back to Josh, grabbed the
microphone and with less than three seconds to go
before the brainwashing effects became permanent
– **KERRUNCH!** – pulverised the microphone.
REARROWWWWWW!!! A
deafening noise reverberated around the theatre.
At once everyone stopped breakdancing and fell
to the floor. A few moments later they came back
to their senses.

Charlie stood up, shaking his head in disbelief.

'W-what just happened?' he said.

Josh patted him on the shoulder. 'You just saved
the world, Charlie – that's what happened!'

'Owww, my head,' the general groaned, trying
to get back to his feet.

Charlie rushed over and picked him up by the
scruff of his neck.

He turned to the audience. 'Ahem, ladies and
gentlemen, for those of you who don't know me,

my name is Hero Boy.' He pushed the general in front of him. 'And for those of you who don't know who Andy Dandy really is . . .' Charlie blew his wig off with a super puff. 'Then let me introduce you to General Pandemonium!'

'AHHHHH . . .' a shocked roar rose up from the audience.

Josh looked at Charlie. 'Okay, so what do we do with the general now?'

Charlie smiled. He reached over and grabbed Josh's iPod. He then pulled the earplugs out of the general's ears and slipped in the iPod's earphones. 'How about we give him a taste of his own medicine?'

Charlie pushed *play* and the general started leaping about crazily on the stage.

'Ha-ha-ha-ha!' the audience exploded with laughter.

Josh held up his mobile phone and started filming. 'Okay, if this doesn't win me first prize in *The World's Wackiest Home Videos*, then nothing will!'

A sea of reporters surged towards Charlie.

'Who are you?' 'Where did you come from?'

'How did you know about the general?' they bellowed, pushing and shoving each other to get near to him.

Just then Grandpa got back to his feet and stumbled awkwardly towards the stage.

'Hey, look – it's Wonder Wally!' one of the reporters shouted. He rushed over to Grandpa. 'Wonder Wally, I can't believe you're still out saving the world at your age! This is incredible! Sir – you're a legend.'

He thrust the microphone into Grandpa's face.

'Wonder Wally, say something to your millions of fans around the world who are no doubt watching this broadcast right now.'

Grandpa screwed up his face.

'*Crikey!* – I think I might have just wet myself!'

GRANDPA'S WONDER DOWN UNDER

'For he's a jolly good fellow . . . for he's a jolly good fellow . . .'

Mum, Dad, Trixie and Charlie sat round the dining table singing a toast to Grandpa at his farewell party.

'Oh, you're too kind,' Grandpa said, wiping his nose. 'All this attention for me? I can't believe it. Oh it's such a thrill to see everyone so excited about my farewell party.'

Mum smiled at Grandpa across the table. 'Trust me, Wallace, I've been counting down the minutes.'

'So, Grandpa, where are you going to live now?' Charlie said.

Grandpa smiled. 'Ah, I'm going to back to my old rest home, but this time things are going to be very different. After proving I've still got a bit of fight left in me, the owners of the rest home have decided to put me in charge of their security team!'

'Hooray!' a small cheer went around the table.

'And . . . get this . . . not only will I be responsible for the rest home's security, I'm also going to be setting up a new iceberg collision prevention programme for them too. Pretty snazzy, eh?'

Charlie looked at Grandpa. 'Um, Grandpa, where did you say your rest home was again?'

'At the Scranton Estate. You know, that old converted castle that backs on to the Halperts' sheep farm.'

'A-ha, I see,' Charlie said. 'Do you think you'll bump into many icebergs on a sheep farm?'

Grandpa wiped his nose again. 'Not if I can help it!'

Mum looked at Charlie. 'So whatever happened to General Pandemonium? I heard he was tied up with that singer Andy Dandy or something?'

'Mum, Andy Dandy *is* General Pandemonium,'

Charlie said. 'He was trying to trick everyone into listening to his music so he could brainwash them. But thanks to us, that super scumbag is in jail now and no one will ever hear from him again.' Charlie put his glass down. 'Although, can you believe it – even though he's in jail, his duet with Hyper Hamster is number one in the charts at the moment!'

Dad smiled. 'Boy oh boy – it just goes to show the old saying is true: any publicity is good publicity in the entertainment industry!'

Grandpa looked at his watch. 'By jingo, is that the time? I'd better skedaddle before the traffic gets too heavy.'

A few moments later Charlie's family assembled on the lawn to wave goodbye to Grandpa.

TOOT-TOOT! He hovered out of the garage on his bright red scooter. 'All right, see you folks another time,' he warbled.

Charlie waved frantically. 'Hey, Grandpa, stop – aren't you forgetting something important?' he asked.

Grandpa shook his head. 'What?'

Charlie pointed at the house. 'Don't you need to go to the loo before your long trip home?'

Grandpa laughed and patted his hips. 'Not any more, I don't. Your mum bought me some special "wonder undies" from the chemist, so now I can "go" wherever I, er, *go*! She said she didn't want anything slowing me down getting home.'

'I wish I hadn't asked,' muttered Charlie, grimacing.

TOOT-TOOT! Grandpa waved goodbye as he rose over the trees and up towards the clouds.

Later that night, for the first time in nearly a month, Charlie jumped into his own bed.

'Ahh, it's good to be back,' he said, pulling the covers up around his ears. He leaned over to switch off his Commander Ron lamp.

But suddenly – 'ARGGGH!!!' – a deafening scream came from the room next door. Trixie ran down the hallway bawling with Mr Tiddlebink bounding along behind her gripping a rubber snake in his jaws.

'Help, someone put a snake in my bed!' she bellowed.

Mum ran into the hallway. 'Trixie? What's happening? Did you say someone put a snake in your bed? I don't understand.'

Mum leaned into Charlie's room. 'Charlie, do you know anything about this? Who on earth would put a snake in Trixie's bed? Everyone knows she's petrified of them.'

Charlie rolled over and closed his eyes. 'Sorry, Mum . . . I have absolutely no idea what you're talking about.'